ALI BABA
AND THE
FORTY THIEVES
AND OTHER
STORIES

Titles in Derrydale's Illustrated Stories for Children Series

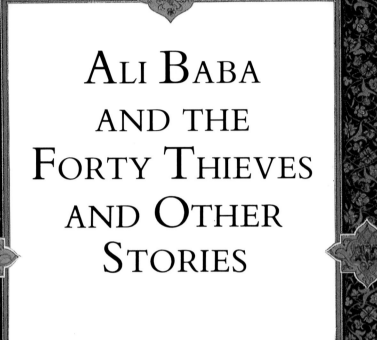

ALI BABA
AND THE
FORTY THIEVES
AND OTHER
STORIES

Illustrated by A. E. Jackson

ILLUSTRATED
STORIES
FOR CHILDREN

DERRYDALE
New York

This 1999 edition is published by Derrydale™,
an imprint of Random House Value Publishing, Inc.,
201 East 50th Street, New York, New York 10022.

Derrydale™ and colophon are trademarks of
Random House Value Publishing, Inc.

Random House
New York • Toronto • London • Sydney • Auckland
http://www.randomhouse.com/

Printed and bound in Singapore

A CIP catalog record for this book is available from the Library of Congress.

Ali Baba and the Forty Thieves and Other Stories / illustrated by A. E. Jackson /
Series: Illustrated Stories for Children
ISBN 0-517-20425-8

8 7 6 5 4 3 2 1

Contents

Introduction

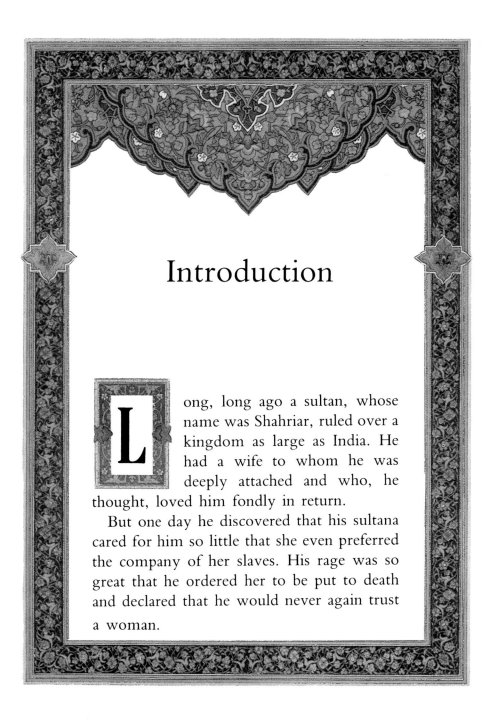

Long, long ago a sultan, whose name was Shahriar, ruled over a kingdom as large as India. He had a wife to whom he was deeply attached and who, he thought, loved him fondly in return.

But one day he discovered that his sultana cared for him so little that she even preferred the company of her slaves. His rage was so great that he ordered her to be put to death and declared that he would never again trust a woman.

Consequently, since the sultan did not care to remain single, he married a new wife every day, and had her put to death the following morning.

Now the grand vizier—that is to say, prime minister—had a beautiful daughter whose name was Sheherazade. In addition to being very beautiful she was very accomplished. She also had an amazing memory and never forgot anything she had read or heard. In fact, she possessed almost every virtue, and was the apple of her father's eye.

One day, when the grand vizier was looking extremely worried because so few suitable young ladies were left for the sultan to marry, his daughter, Sheherazade, came to him and said, "My father, I have a favor to ask."

"Ask, my child," he replied, "and if the request is reasonable, which, coming from you, it is sure to be, you may consider it granted."

"Then, my dear father," said Sheherazade, "let *me* be the sultan's next wife."

The grand vizier was at first struck dumb and breathless with horror. When he had recovered, he did his best to persuade his daughter to change her mind. But Sheherazade persisted and begged and coaxed the poor man until, much against his will, he agreed that she should have her way.

Even the sultan himself was surprised when the grand vizier proposed the match; for, as he plainly told his minister, his daughter must not expect to escape the fate which had befallen all the wives who had preceded her.

The grand vizier, with tears in his eyes, replied that both he and his daughter were well aware of this, but that they would, nevertheless, regard the temporary alliance as a great honor.

"In that case," said the sultan, "the marriage can take place tomorrow."

So, Sheherazade, gorgeously arrayed, was led to the palace and the marriage took place.

Now, as before mentioned, Sheherazade was extremely beautiful, and the sultan was quite charmed with her, and felt almost sorry that he would have to order her to be put to death in the usual way.

The day was just beginning to break when Sheherazade said, "I wonder if His Imperial Highness would allow me to relate one of my stories? Please let me tell one more tale before my lips are closed forever."

"What is that?" asked the sultan sleepily. "Let you tell a story? Why, certainly."

10

At first he did not pay very much attention to the tale. But, as it went on, he became so enthralled that he felt he simply *must* hear the end. So, since it was time for him to rise and attend to affairs of state, he decided to put off the execution of Sheherazade for another twenty-four hours, or more if required.

The story of "Ali Baba and the Forty Thieves," and the others that follow, were among the tales told by Sheherazade during the "thousand and one nights," for each successive night brought a story as wonderful as those that had gone before. The sultan eventually fell in love with the fair storyteller and had not the heart to kill her. And everyone will agree that, had he done so, he would have been not only a very wicked but a very foolish man.

Ali Baba
and the Forty Thieves

I n a town in Persia there lived
two brothers, one named Cassim, the other Ali Baba. When
their father died, what little
property he had was equally divided between his two sons. Cassim, however, married the daughter of a rich merchant
and soon became the owner of a fine shop
and several pieces of land. Consequently,
through no effort of his own, he became one
of the richest merchants in the town.

Ali Baba, on the other hand, married a woman he loved, who was as poor as himself, and had to eke out a living by cutting wood in a neighboring forest, loading it on his three donkeys, which were his only possession, and selling it about the town.

One day Ali Baba went to the forest and had almost finished cutting as much wood as his donkeys could carry when he saw coming toward him a large company of horsemen. He feared from their appearance that they might be robbers. He was a cautious man, so he climbed a tree that grew at the foot of a large rock and hid himself among the branches, where he could see without being seen.

Almost immediately it became evident that this very rock was the destination toward which the troop was bound. When they arrived each man alighted instantly from his horse, tethered it, and removed a sack that seemed by its weight and form to be filled with gold. There could no longer be any doubt that they were robbers. Ali Baba counted forty of them.

Just as he had done so, the man nearest to him, who seemed to be their leader, advanced toward the rock, and in a low but distinct voice uttered two words, "Open, Sesame!" Immediately the rock opened like a door, the leader and his men passed in, and the rock closed behind them.

For a long time Ali Baba waited. He didn't dare to descend from his hiding place lest they come out and catch him in the act. At last, when the waiting had grown almost unbearable, his patience was rewarded. The door in the rock opened, and out came the forty men, their captain leading them. When the last of them was through, the leader said, "Shut, Sesame!" and immediately the face of the rock closed together as before. Then they all mounted their horses and rode away.

As soon as he felt sure that they were not returning, Ali Baba came down from the tree and made his way to that part of the rock where he had seen the captain and his men enter. He remembered

the words the captain had said and wondered what would happen if he said them. "Open, Sesame!" he exclaimed, and the rock suddenly flew open.

Ali Baba, who had expected to find only a dark and gloomy cave, was astonished to see a large, spacious, well-lighted vaulted room, dug out of the rock and so high that he could not touch the ceiling with his hand. Light came in from an opening at the top of the rock. He saw in it a large quantity of provisions, numerous bales of rich merchandise, a store of silks and brocades, and, besides all this, great quantities of coins, both silver and gold, some piled in heaps and the rest stored in large leather bags placed one on top of another.

Ali Baba did not hesitate for a moment, but entered the cave. As soon as he was in, the door closed behind him. But, since he knew the magic words by which to open it, this did not worry him. He paid no attention to the silver, but went directly for the gold coins, and particularly the portion that was in the bags. Having collected as much as he thought he could carry, he went out in search of his donkeys, which he had left to look after themselves when he climbed the tree. They had strayed some way, but he brought them close to the opening in the rock. He loaded them with the sacks of gold and covered the sacks with wood so that they might not be seen. Then he closed the rock by saying the magic words he had learned, and departed for the town, a well-satisfied man.

When he got home he drove his donkeys into a small court. Shutting the gates carefully, he took off the wood that covered the bags and carried them in to his wife. She, discovering them to be full of gold, was afraid that her husband had stolen them and began sorrowfully to reproach him. Ali Baba soon put her mind at rest and, having poured all the gold into a great heap upon the floor, he sat down at her side to consider how wonderful it looked.

Soon his wife began counting the gold piece by piece. Ali Baba let her go on for a while, then he began laughing. "Wife," he said,

"you will never finish it that way. The best thing to do is to dig a hole and bury it, then we shall be sure that it is not slipping through our fingers."

"That will do well enough," said his wife, "but it would be better first to know how much gold is here. While you dig the hole I will go to Cassim's and borrow a measure small enough to give us an exact reckoning."

"Do as you will," answered her husband, "but see that you keep the thing secret."

Off went Ali Baba's wife to her brother-in-law's house. Cassim was away from home, so she asked his wife to lend her a small measure. This set the sister-in-law wondering. Knowing Ali Baba's poverty she was all the more curious to find out what kind of grain would require so small a measure. So before bringing it she covered the bottom with lard, and giving it to Ali Baba's wife told her to be sure to be quick in returning it. Ali Baba's wife agreed and made haste to get home; there finding the hole dug for its reception, she started to measure the gold into it. First she set the measure upon the heap, then she filled it, then she carried it to the hole; and so she continued until the last measure was counted. Then, leaving Ali Baba to finish the burying, she carried back the measure with all haste to her sister-in-law.

No sooner was her back turned than Cassim's wife looked at the bottom of the measure, and there to her astonishment she saw sticking to the lard a gold coin. "What!" she exclaimed, "has Ali Baba such an abundance of gold that he measures it instead of counting it? If that is so, how in the world did he get it?"

The moment her husband, Cassim, entered the house his wife flew to him and said, "Cassim, you think you are rich, but Ali Baba has infinitely more wealth; he does not count his gold as you do, he measures it." Cassim demanded an explanation, and his wife showed him the piece of gold she had found sticking to the bottom of the measure.

Far from feeling any pleasure at his brother's good fortune, Cassim was extremely jealous. The next morning, before sunrise, he went to Ali Baba with the intention of solving the mystery.

"Oh, Ali Baba," he said, "you are very reserved in your affairs. You pretend to be poor and yet you have so much money that you must measure it."

"Oh, my brother," replied Ali Baba, "I do not understand. Please explain what you mean."

"Do not pretend ignorance," answered Cassim, and he showed Ali Baba the piece of gold his wife had given him. "How many pieces have you like this that my wife found sticking to the bottom of the measure that your wife borrowed yesterday?"

17

Ali Baba, realizing that further concealment was useless, told his brother exactly what had happened and offered him an equal share of the treasure.

"That is the least that I have the right to expect," answered Cassim haughtily. "But you must also tell me exactly where the treasure lies so I may, if necessary, test the truth of your story. Otherwise I shall find it my duty to denounce you to the authorities."

Ali Baba, having a clear conscience, had little fear of Cassim's threats. But out of pure good nature he gave him all the information he desired, not forgetting to instruct him in the words that would permit him to get into the cave and out again.

Cassim, who had thus got all he had come for, lost no time in putting his own plan into execution. Intent on possessing all the treasures that yet remained he set off the next morning before daybreak, taking with him ten mules laden with empty crates. When he arrived at the rock, he remembered the words his brother had taught him. No sooner was "Open, Sesame!" said that the door in the rock opened wide for him to pass through. And when he had entered, it shut behind him.

If the simple soul of Ali Baba had found delight in the riches of the cavern, greater still was the exultation of a greedy nature like Cassim's. Drunk with the wealth that lay before his eyes, all he could think of was gathering with all speed as much treasure as the ten mules could carry. Finally, having exhausted himself with heavy labor and greedy excitement, he suddenly found on returning to the door that he had forgotten the magic words.

"Open, Barley!" he said, but the door did not bulge an inch. He then named the various other kinds of grain, all but the right one, but the door did not move.

The more he tried to remember the word *sesame,* the more he failed. He threw to the ground the sacks he had collected, and paced

backward and forward in a frenzy of terror. The riches that surrounded him no longer had any attraction for him.

Toward noon the robbers returned, and saw, standing about the rock, the ten mules laden with crates. They were greatly surprised, and began to search with suspicion among the surrounding crannies and undergrowth. Finding no one there, they drew their swords and advanced cautiously toward the cave.

Cassim, who from within had heard the trampling of horses, now had no doubt that the robbers were back and that they would kill him. Resolved however to make one last effort at escape, he stood ready by the door. No sooner had the opening word been uttered than he ran forward with such violence that he threw the captain to the ground. But his attempt was in vain. Before he could break through he was mercilessly killed by the swords of the robber band.

When the robbers entered the cave they immediately found the sacks of gold that Cassim had left near the entrance, and replaced them. But they did not notice the absence of those taken by Ali Baba. They were, however, puzzled as to the means by which Cassim had managed to enter the cave. To scare off anyone else who might dare to enter, they cut the body of the unfortunate Cassim into quarters, and placed them near the door.

Then they mounted their horses, and set off to commit more robberies.

Meanwhile, Cassim's wife had grown very uneasy at her husband's failure to return. Finally, at nightfall, unable to endure further suspense, she ran to Ali Baba, told him of his brother's secret expedition, and begged him to go out instantly in search of him.

Ali Baba had too kind a heart to refuse her. Taking with him his three donkeys he set out immediately for the forest. Since the road was familiar to him he soon found his way to the door of the cave. When he saw there the traces of blood he became filled with misgiving, but no sooner had he entered than his worst fears were

realized. Nevertheless, brotherly love and respect gave him courage. Gathering together the severed remains and wrapping them
gently, he placed them upon one of the donkeys and concealed
them with wood. Then thinking that he deserved some payment for
his trouble he loaded the two remaining donkeys with sacks of
gold, and, covering them with wood as he had on the first occasion, he made his way back to town while it was yet early.

21

Leaving his wife to take care of the treasure borne by the two donkeys, Ali Baba led the third to his sister-in-law's house. Knocking quietly so that none of the neighbors might hear, he was presently admitted by Morgiana, a female slave whose intelligence and discretion had long been known to him.

"Morgiana," he said, "there's trouble on the back of that donkey. Can you keep a secret?"

Morgiana's nod satisfied him better than any oath.

"Well," he said, "your master's body lies there, and our business now is to bury him honorably as though he had died a natural death. Go and tell your mistress that I want to speak to her."

When Ali Baba's sister-in-law came to him in great anxiety, he first made her promise to listen calmly to the story he had to tell, and then related all that had happened. "Sister," he added, "you must control your grief and do your crying later. We must contrive to bury my brother as though he had died a natural death. I have an idea which, I think, with the help of Morgiana, can be carried out."

At this, Cassim's widow allowed her sobs to subside, for she was not without common sense, and listened while Ali Baba coached Morgiana in the part she was to play.

Accordingly, Morgiana assumed a woeful expression and went to the shop of the nearest apothecary, where she asked for a particular medicine which was supposed to cure the most serious ailments.

On the following day Morgiana again went to the apothecary and, with tears in her eyes, asked for an essence that was customarily administered only when the patient was reduced to the last extremity and no other remedy had been left untried.

"Alas!" she cried, as she received it from the apothecary, "I fear this remedy will be of no more use than the other, and I shall lose my beloved master!"

Since Ali Baba and his wife were seen going to and from the house of Cassim in the course of the day, with very long faces, no one was surprised when, toward evening, the piercing cries of the widow and Morgiana announced his death. And when a sound of wailing arose within the house all the neighbors concluded without further question that Cassim had died a natural and honorable death.

But Morgiana had now a still more difficult task to perform, it being necessary for the funeral that the body be made in some way presentable. Very early the next morning she went to the shop of an old cobbler who lived some distance off. Coming up to him, she wished him good day and put a piece of gold in his hand.

Baba Mustapha, a man well known throughout the city, was by nature of a gay turn of mind, and had always something laughable to say. He examined the piece of money, and seeing that it was gold, said, "This is good wage; what is to be done? I am ready to do your bidding."

"Baba Mustapha," said Morgiana to him, "take all your materials for sewing, and come with me. But I insist on this condition, that you let me cover your eyes until we have reached our destination."

Baba Mustapha began to object. "Oh, ho!" said he, "you want me to do something against my conscience or my honor."

But Morgiana interrupted him by putting another piece of gold in his hand. "Allah forbid," she said, "that I should require you to do anything that would hurt your conscience or stain your honor. Come with me and fear nothing."

Baba Mustapha allowed himself to be led by Morgiana, who bound a handkerchief over his eyes, and brought him to Cassim's house. She did not remove the bandage until he was in the room where the remains were placed. Then, taking off the covering, she said, "Baba Mustapha. I have brought you here so that you may sew these four quarters together. Lose no time. And when you have finished I will give you another piece of gold."

When Baba Mustapha had completed his gruesome task, Morgiana bound his eyes again, and, after giving him the third piece of money, according to her promise, and begging him to keep her secret, she conducted him to the place where she had first put on the handkerchief. Here she uncovered his eyes, and left him to return to his house, watching him, however, until he was out of sight, lest he have the curiosity to return and follow her.

Then the body of the unfortunate Cassim was washed, perfumed, wrapped in an elegant shroud, and buried with due ceremony.

The widow remained at home to lament and weep with the women of the neighborhood, who, according to custom, had repaired to her house during the ceremony. But Morgiana followed the coffin, weeping and tearing her hair.

Ali Baba had a son who had served his apprenticeship with a merchant of good repute. He now put the young man in charge of the shop that had belonged to Cassim, while he himself moved with his belongings to his late brother's house, which was larger and more commodious than his own.

Leaving Ali Baba to enjoy his good fortune, we will now return to the forty thieves. On returning to the cave they were amazed and

alarmed to find the body of Cassim gone, together with a large portion of their treasure.

"We have been discovered," said the captain, "and if we are not very careful, we shall lose all the riches we have gathered with so much trouble and work. All we know is that the thief whom we surprised when he was going to make his escape knew the secret of opening the door. But evidently he was not the only one. Another must have the same knowledge. And, since we have no reason to suppose that more than two people are acquainted with the secret, having destroyed one, we must not allow the other to escape. What say you, my brave comrades?"

The other thirty-nine robbers agreed that it would be advisable to give up every other enterprise, and occupy themselves solely with this affair until they had succeeded.

"Then," resumed the captain, "the first thing to be done is that one of you who is bold, courageous, and cunning should go to the city, unarmed and in the dress of a traveler, and employ all his art to discover if the death we inflicted on the culprit we destroyed is being talked about. Then he must find out who this man was, and where he lived. But, to prevent his bringing us a false report, which might occasion our total ruin, I propose that the one selected to perform the task shall consent to the penalty of death in case of failure."

Without waiting until his companions should speak, one of the robbers said, "I agree to those terms. If I should fail, you will, at least, remember that I displayed both courage and readiness in my offer to serve the troop."

Amid the commendations of the captain and his companions, the robber disguised himself in such a way that no one could have suspected him of being what he was. He set off at night, and entering the city just as day was dawning, went toward the public bazaar, where he saw only one shop open. It was the shop of Baba Mustapha.

26

The merry cobbler was seated on his stool ready to begin work. The robber went up to him and wished him a good morning, saying, "My good man, you rise early to your work. Does not so dull a light strain your eyes?"

"Not so much as you might think," answered Baba Mustapha. "Why, it was only the other day that at this same hour I saw well enough to stitch up a dead body in a place where it was certainly no lighter."

"Stitch up a dead body!" cried the robber, in pretended amazement, concealing his joy at this sudden intelligence. "Surely you mean in its shroud, for how else can a dead body be stitched?"

"No, no," said Mustapha. "What I say I mean. But since it is a secret, I can tell you no more."

The robber drew out a piece of gold. "Come," he said, "tell me nothing you do not care to. Only show me the house where lay the body that you stitched."

Baba Mustapha eyed the gold longingly. "Would that I could," he replied. "But alas! I went to it blindfolded."

"Well," said the robber, "I have heard that a blind man remembers his road. Perhaps, though seeing you might lose it, blindfolded you might find it again."

Tempted by the offer of yet another piece of gold, Baba Mustapha was soon persuaded to make the attempt. "It was here that I started," he said, showing the spot, "and I turned as you see me now." The robber then put a handkerchief over his eyes and walked beside him through the streets, partly guiding and partly being led, until of his own accord Baba Mustapha stopped. "It was here," he said. "The door by which I went in should now lie to the right." And he had in fact come exactly opposite the house which had once been Cassim's and where Ali Baba now dwelt.

The robber marked the door with a piece of chalk that he had brought for the purpose. He removed the handkerchief from Mustapha's eyes and left him to his own devices, then returned with

all possible speed to the cave where his comrades were awaiting him.

Soon after the robber and cobbler had parted, Morgiana happened to go out on an errand, and as she returned she noticed the mark upon the door.

This, she thought, is not as it should be. Either some trick is intended, or there is evil brewing for my master's house. Taking a piece of chalk she put a similar mark upon the five or six doors lying to right and left. And having done this she went home with her mind satisfied, saying nothing.

In the meantime the robbers had learned from their companion about the success of his venture. Greatly elated at the thought of the vengeance so soon to be theirs, they formed a plan for entering the city in a manner that should arouse no suspicion among the inhabitants. Passing in by twos and threes, and by different routes, they met at the marketplace at an appointed time while the captain and the robber who had acted as spy made their way alone to the street where the marked door was to be found.

Presently, just as they had expected, they saw a door with the mark on it.

"That is it!" said the robber, but as they continued walking to avoid suspicion, they came upon another marked door and another, until they had passed six in succession. So alike were the marks that the spy, though he swore he had made only one, could not tell which it was.

The captain was very annoyed, but there was nothing to do but return to the forest, where the unlucky robber had his head cut off as the penalty for his failure.

In spite of this, another robber, who flattered himself with hopes of greater success, asked to be allowed to see what he could do. Permission was granted, so he went to the city, bribed Baba Mustapha with more gold, and the cobbler, with his eyes bound, went

through the same performance and led him to the house of Ali Baba.

The thief marked the door with red chalk in a place where it would be less noticed, thinking this would be a surer method of distinguishing it. But a short time afterward Morgiana went out, as on the preceding day, and on her return the red mark did not escape her sharp eyes. She immediately made a similar mark on all the neighboring doors.

When he returned to his companions in the forest, the thief boasted of the precautions he had taken to distinguish the house of Ali Baba, to which he offered to lead the captain without fail. But the result was the same. A whole row of front doors marked with red chalk met the captain's irritated eye; and the second robber lost *his* head.

This reduced the forty thieves to thirty-eight, and the captain decided to undertake the task himself. He returned to the city and, with the assistance of Baba Mustapha, found Ali Baba's house. But, having no faith in chalk marks, he imprinted the place thoroughly on his memory, looking at it so attentively that he was certain he could not mistake it.

He then returned to the forest, and when he had reached the cave said, "Comrades, I know with certainty the house of the culprit who is to experience our revenge, and I have planned an excellent way of dealing with him."

He then ordered them to divide into small parties, which were to go into the neighboring towns and villages and there buy nineteen mules and thirty-eight large leather jars for carrying oil. One of the jars must be full, and all the others empty.

In the course of two or three days the thieves completed their purchases to the captain's satisfaction. He made one of the men, thoroughly armed, enter each jar. He then closed the jars, so that they appeared to be full of oil, leaving, however, a sufficient space to admit air for the men to breathe. And, the better to carry out the

deception, he rubbed the outside of each jar with oil, which he took from the full one.

Thus prepared, the mules were laden with the thirty-seven robbers, each concealed in a jar, and with the jar that was filled with oil. Then the captain, disguised as an oil merchant, took the road to the city, where the whole procession arrived about an hour after sunset.

The captain went straight to the house of Ali Baba, intending to knock and request shelter for the night for himself and his mules. He was, however, spared the trouble of knocking, for he found Ali Baba at the door, enjoying the fresh air after supper. Addressing him in tones of respect, the captain said, "Sir, I have brought my oil a great distance to sell tomorrow in the market. And at this late hour, being a stranger, I do not know where to seek shelter. If it is not troubling you too much, allow me to stable my beasts here for the night."

The captain's voice was now so changed from its accustomed tone of command that Ali Baba, although he had heard it before, did not recognize it. Not only did he grant the stranger's request for bare accommodation, but as soon as the unloading and stabling of the mules had been accomplished, he invited him to stay not in the outer court but in the house as his guest. The captain, whose plans this proposal somewhat disarranged, tried to excuse himself. But since Ali Baba would take no refusal he was forced at last to yield, and to submit with apparent pleasure to some entertainment, which the hospitality of his host extended to a late hour.

When they were about to retire for the night, Ali Baba went into the kitchen to speak to Morgiana. The captain of the robbers, on the pretext of going to look after his mules, slipped out into the yard where the oil jars were standing in line. Passing from jar to jar he whispered into each, "When you hear a handful of pebbles fall from the window of the room where I am lodged, cut your way out of the jar and make ready, for the time will have come." He

then returned to the house, where Morgiana came with a light and conducted him to his chamber.

Now Ali Baba, before going to bed, had said to Morgiana, "To-morrow at dawn I am going to the baths. Let my bathing linen be put ready, and see that the cook has some good broth prepared for me when I return." Having therefore led the guest up to his room, Morgiana returned to the kitchen and ordered Abdallah the cook to put on the pot for the broth. Suddenly, while Morgiana was skimming it, the lamp went out, and, on searching, she found there was no more oil in the house. At so late an hour no shop would be open, yet somehow the broth had to be made, and that could not be done without a light.

"As for that," said Abdallah, seeing her perplexity, "why trouble yourself? There is plenty of oil out in the yard."

"Why, to be sure!" said Morgiana, and sending Abdallah to bed so that he might be up in time to wake his master in the morning, she took the oil can herself and went out into the court. As she approached the jar which stood nearest, she heard a voice within say, "Is it time?"

To one of Morgiana's intelligence an oil jar that spoke was an object of even more suspicion than a chalk mark on a door. In an instant she realized what danger for her master and his family might lie concealed around her. Understanding well enough that an oil jar that asked a question required an answer, she replied quick as thought and without the least sign of perturbation, "Not yet, but presently." And thus she passed from jar to jar, thirty-seven in all, giving the same answer, until she came to the one which contained the oil.

The situation was now clear to her. Aware of the source from which her master had acquired his wealth, she guessed at once that, in extending shelter to the oil merchant, Ali Baba had actually admitted to his house the robber captain and his band. She immediately knew what she had to do. Having filled the oil can she

returned to the kitchen. There she lighted the lamp, and then, taking a large kettle, went back once more to the jar that contained the oil. Filling the kettle she carried it back to the kitchen, and putting under it a great fire of wood had soon brought it to the boil. Then lifting it once more, she went out into the yard and poured into each jar in turn a sufficient quantity of the boiling oil to scald its occupant to death.

She then returned to the kitchen and, having made Ali Baba's broth, put out the fire, blew out the lamp, and sat down by the window to watch.

Before long the captain of the robbers awoke from the short sleep he had allowed himself. Finding that all was silent in the house, he rose softly and opened the window. Below stood the oil jars. Gently into their midst he threw the handful of pebbles agreed on as a signal. But from the oil jars there came no answer. He threw a second and a third time. Though he could hear the pebbles falling among the jars, there followed only the silence of the dead. Wondering whether his band had fled, leaving him in the lurch, or whether they were all asleep, he grew uneasy, and descending in haste, he made his way into the court. As he approached the first jar a smell of burning and hot oil assailed his nostrils, and looking within he beheld the dead body of his comrade.

In every jar the same sight presented itself until he came to the one that contained the oil. There, in what was missing, the means and manner of his companions' death were made clear to him. Aghast at the discovery and awake to the danger that now threatened him, he did not delay an instant, but forcing the garden gate open, and from there climbing from wall to wall, he made his escape out of the city.

When Morgiana, who had remained on the watch all this time, was assured of his final departure, she got her master's bath linen ready and went to bed well satisfied with her day's work.

The next morning Ali Baba, awakened by his slave, went to the

baths before daybreak. On his return he was greatly surprised to find that the merchant was gone, leaving his mules and oil jars behind him. He asked Morgiana the reason.

"You will find the reason," said she, "if you look into the first jar you come to."

Ali Baba did so, and, seeing a man, started back with a cry.

"Do not be afraid," said Morgiana, "he is dead and harmless. And so are all the others whom you will find if you look further."

As Ali Baba went from one jar to another, finding always the same sight of horror within, his knees trembled under him. When he came at last to the one empty oil jar, he stood for a time motionless, turning upon Morgiana eyes of wonder and inquiry. "And what," he said then, "has become of the merchant?"

"To tell you that," said Morgiana, "will be to tell you the whole story. You will be better able to hear it if you have your broth first."

But Ali Baba's curiosity was far too great. He would not be kept waiting. So without further delay Morgiana told him everything, so far as she knew it, from beginning to end. And by her intelligent putting of one thing against another, she left him at last in no possible doubt as to the source and nature of the conspiracy that her quick wits had so happily defeated.

"And now, dear master," she said in conclusion, "continue to be on your guard, for though all these are dead, one remains alive. And he, if I am not mistaken, is the captain of the band, and for that reason is the more formidable and the more likely to cherish the hope of vengeance."

When Morgiana had finished speaking Ali Baba realized that he owed to her not merely the protection of his property, but life itself. He was full of gratitude. "Do not doubt," he said "that before I die I will reward you as you deserve. And as an immediate proof, from this moment I give you your liberty."

This token of his approval filled Morgiana's heart with delight,

but she had no intention of leaving so kind a master, even had she been sure that all danger was now over. The immediate question that presented itself was how to dispose of the bodies.

Luckily, at the far end of the garden there stood a thick grove of trees. Under these Ali Baba was able to dig a large trench without attracting the notice of his neighbors. Here the remains of the thirty-seven robbers were laid side by side, the trench was filled again, and the ground made level. As for the mules, since Ali Baba had no use for them, he sent them, one or two at a time, to the market to be sold.

Meanwhile the robber captain had fled back to the forest. Entering the cave he was overcome by its gloom and loneliness. "Alas!" he cried, "my comrades, partners in my adventures, sharers of my fortune, how shall I endure to live without you? Why did I lead you to a fate where bravery was of no avail, and where death turned you into objects of ridicule? Surely had you died sword in hand my sorrow would be less bitter! And now what remains for me but to take vengeance for your death and to prove, by achieving it without aid, that I was worthy to be the captain of such a band!"

Thus decided, at an early hour the next day, he assumed a disguise suitable to his purpose, and going to the town took lodging in an inn. Entering into conversation with his host he inquired whether anything of interest had happened recently in the town. But the other man, though full of gossip, had nothing to tell him concerning the matter in which he was most interested, for Ali Baba, having to conceal from all the source of his wealth, had also to be silent as to the dangers in which it involved him.

The captain then inquired where there was a shop for rent. Hearing of one that suited him, he came to terms with the owner, and before long had furnished it with all kinds of rich stuffs and carpets and jewelry which he brought gradually and with great secrecy from the cave.

This shop happened to be opposite the one that had belonged to

Cassim and was now occupied by the son of Ali Baba. Before long the son and the newcomer, who had assumed the name of Cogia Houssain, became acquainted. Since the youth had good looks, kind manners, and a sociable disposition, it was not long before they became close friends.

Cogia Houssain did all he could to seal the pretended friendship, particularly since it had not taken him long to discover how the young man and Ali Baba were related. So, plying him constantly with small presents and acts of hospitality, he forced on him the obligation of making some return.

Ali Baba's son, however, had not at his lodging sufficent accommodation for entertainment. He therefore told his father of the difficulty in which Cogia Houssain's favors had placed him. Ali Baba with great willingness at once offered to arrange matters. "My son," he said, "tomorrow being a holiday, all shops will be closed. After dinner invite Cogia Houssain to walk with you and as you return bring him this way and beg him to come in. That will be better than a formal invitation, and Morgiana shall have supper prepared for you."

This proposal was exactly what Ali Baba's son could have wished. The next day he brought Cogia Houssain to the door as if by accident, and stopping, invited him to enter.

Cogia Houssain, who saw that he was getting just what he wanted, began by showing pretended reluctance, but Ali Baba himself came to the door, urged him in the most kindly manner to enter, and before long had led him to the table where food stood prepared.

But then an unforeseen difficulty arose. Wicked though he might be the robber captain was not so impious as to eat the salt of the man he intended to kill. He therefore began to excuse himself with many apologies. When Ali Baba sought to know the reason, "Sir," he said, "I am sure that if you knew the cause of my resolution you would approve of it. Suffice it to say that I have made it a rule to eat of no dish that has salt in it. How then can I sit down at your table if I must reject everything that is set before me?"

"If that is your scruple," said Ali Baba, "it shall soon be satisfied," and he sent orders to the kitchen that no salt was to be put into any of the dishes to be served to the newly arrived guest.

"Thus," he said to Cogia Houssain, "I shall still have the honor, to which I have looked forward, of returning to you under my own roof the hospitality you have shown my son."

Morgiana, who was just about to serve supper, received the order with some discontent. "Who," she said, "is this difficult person who refuses to eat salt? He must be a curiosity worth looking at." So when the saltless courses were ready to be set upon the table, she herself helped to carry in the dishes. No sooner had she set eyes on Cogia Houssain than she recognized him in spite of his disguise. Observing his movements with great attention she saw that he had a dagger concealed beneath his robe.

"Ah!" she said to herself, "here is reason enough! For who will eat salt with the man he means to murder? But he shall not murder my master if I can prevent it."

Now Morgiana knew that the most favorable opportunity for the robber captain to carry out his plan would be after the food had been withdrawn, and when Ali Baba and his son and guest were alone together drinking their wine. This was indeed the very plan that Cogia Houssain had made. Going out quickly, Morgiana dressed herself as a dancer, assuming the appropriate headdress and mask. Then she fastened a silver girdle about her waist, and hung upon it a dagger of the same material. Thus equipped, she said to Abdallah the cook, "Take your tabor and let us go in and give an entertainment in honor of our master's guest."

So Abdallah took his tabor, and played Morgiana into the hall. As soon as she had entered she made a low curtsy, and stood awaiting orders. Then Ali Baba, seeing that she wished to perform in his guest's honor, said kindly, "Come in, Morgiana, and show Cogia Houssain what you can do."

Immediately Abdallah began to beat upon his tabor and sing an air for Morgiana to dance to. And she, advancing with much grace, began to move through several figures, performing them with the ease and facility that none but the most highly practiced can attain.

Then, for the last figure of all, she drew out the dagger and, holding it in her hand, danced a dance that excelled all that had preceded it in the surprise and change and quickness and dexterity of its movements. Now she presented the dagger at her own breast, now

at one of the onlookers; but always in the act of striking she drew back. Finally, as though out of breath, she snatched his instrument from Abdallah with her left hand, and, still holding the dagger in her right, advanced the hollow of her tabor toward her master, as is the custom of dancers when claiming their fee. Ali Baba threw in a piece of gold. His son did the same. Then advancing it in the same manner toward Cogia Houssain, who was feeling for his purse she struck under it, and before he knew had plunged her dagger deep into his heart.

Ali Baba and his son, seeing their guest fall dead, cried out in horror. "Wretch!" exclaimed Ali Baba, "what ruin and shame have you brought on us?"

"No," answered Morgiana, "it is not your ruin but your life that I have saved. Look closely at this man who refused to eat salt with you!" So saying, she tore off the dead robber's disguise, showing the dagger concealed below, and the face which her master now recognized for the first time.

Ali Baba's gratitude to Morgiana for preserving his life a second time knew no bounds. He took her in his arms and embraced her as a daughter. "Now," he said, "the time has come when I must fulfill my debt and how better can I do it than by marrying you to my son?" This proposition, far from proving unwelcome to the young man, did but confirm an inclination already formed. A few days later the nuptials were celebrated with great joy and solemnity, and the union thus auspiciously commenced was productive of as much happiness as lies within the power of mortals to secure.

As for the robbers' cave, it remained the secret possession of Ali Baba and his posterity; and using their good fortune with equity and moderation, they rose to high office in the city and were held in great honor by all who knew them.

The
Enchanted Horse

Once upon a time there was a King of Persia named Sabur. He had one son and one daughter. The son, Feroze-shah, was the apple of his father's eye, and, indeed, he was the handsomest, bravest, and most amiable prince in all the world.

On the first day of the year, which was observed as a festival, the king always held a public audience at which he received gifts and congratulations, and bestowed pardons and rewards.

On one of these occasions, a Hindu presented himself before the king with a magnificent horse made of ebony and inlaid with ivory. This horse was so beautifully sculpted that it almost seemed alive.

The king was delighted with it and immediately offered to buy it.

But the Hindu, prostrating himself before the king, explained that this was an enchanted horse, which would carry its rider wherever he wished to go, in the shortest possible time. He added that he was willing to part with the horse on only one condition. But, before stating that condition, he would give an exhibition of the horse's powers.

"Then mount," said the king, "and bring me a branch of the palm tree which grows at the foot of yonder hill." And he pointed to a hill about three leagues away.

The Hindu mounted and, turning a peg on the right side of the horse's neck, was instantly borne upward and carried through the air at a great height and with the speed of lightning, to the amazement of all beholders.

In less than a quarter of an hour he was back with the palm branch, which, on dismounting, he laid at the feet of the king. The king's desire to possess this magic steed was now increased a hundred times, and he offered to pay whatever sum the other demanded.

"Sire," replied the Hindu, "there is only one thing I will take in exchange for this horse, which, as your Majesty perceives, is one of the wonders of the world."

"What is that?" inquired the king. "Name it and it is yours."

"The hand of the princess, your daughter," was the reply, which excited the ridicule of all who heard—for the Hindu was not only unpleasant in appearance, but was at least twice the age of the king. And the princess, who was only fifteen, was as beautiful as she was charming.

44

Prince Feroze-shah, who stood beside the King, his father, was extremely indignant.

"I hope, my father," he said, "that you will not hesitate to refuse such an insolent demand."

"My son," replied the king, who had a craving for anything that was rare and curious, "I have no intention of granting the request. But, perhaps, he is not serious in making it, and would accept the weight of the horse in gold. In any case, suppose you mount the horse yourself and give me your opinion of it."

The prince was all too willing to agree and the Hindu ran to assist him. But the prince mounted without his help and as soon as he had his feet in the stirrups, without waiting for instructions, he turned the peg as he had seen the other do. Instantly, the horse rose in the air, as swift as an arrow, and in a few moments both horse and rider were out of sight.

The Hindu, alarmed at what had happened, prostrated himself before the king, who was angry and distressed at the disappearance of his son.

"Your Majesty must admit that I was blameless," he said. "The prince gave me no time to utter a word, or to point out to him a second peg by which the horse is controlled and made to descend. It can also be guided by means of the bridle. But it is possible that the prince may discover this for himself."

"Your own life shall answer for that of my son," said the king. "And until he returns, or I hear some tidings of him, you shall be put in prison and fed on bread and water."

Meanwhile, the prince was being carried so rapidly through the air that in less than an hour he was out of sight of the earth. He then thought it was time to return. He pulled the bridle and grabbed the peg with which he had started the horse. He turned the peg the opposite way. When he found that this had no effect, but that the horse continued to ascend, he became alarmed. He continued to turn the peg one way and another, but without arresting the horse's

ascent. It seemed as though, in time, he would be burnt up by the sun. Then, to his great joy and relief, he discovered another, smaller peg behind the horse's other ear. Turning this, his upward flight was instantly checked and he began to descend, but at a much slower rate.

The sun was already setting. It grew dark rapidly as he drew near the earth, so that he was unable to discover what was beneath him—whether a city, a desert, a plain, or a mountain top. It was equally possible that the horse might plunge with him into a lake or a river, or even into the sea. Consequently, when at the dead of night the horse at last came to a stop, and the prince felt solid ground beneath his feet, he was inexpressibly relieved. He was also agreeably surprised to find himself on the terrace of a magnificent palace, gleaming with white marble.

He was faint and hungry, having eaten nothing since the early morning, and at first could scarcely stand. But, leaving the horse, he groped his way along until he came to a staircase, which he found led downward. At the foot of the stairs there was a half-open door, through which a ray of light shone.

Descending as noiselessly as possible, the prince paused at the door and, listening, heard the loud breathing of sleepers within. He advanced cautiously, and by the light of a lamp saw that the sleepers were guards. Their naked sabers lay beside them, and he realized that this was the guard chamber of some royal personage.

Proceeding on tiptoe, the prince crossed the room, without waking any of the sleepers, to a curtained archway. Raising the curtain, he saw a magnificent chamber with a raised couch in the center. Around the sides of the chamber were low couches on which a number of female servants were sleeping. The prince crept softly toward the center couch, and saw the most beautiful princess in the world sleeping on her silken pillows, her hair spread round her like a veil.

Falling on his knees, he remained entranced by her loveliness until the power of his gaze penetrated her closed eyelids, and, opening her eyes, she saw the handsomest prince in the world regarding her in an ecstasy of admiration.

She showed the greatest surprise, but not the least sign of fear. The prince ventured to address her in the most respectful manner.

"Beautiful Princess," he said, "you see at your feet the Prince of Persia, brought here by what he now regards as a most happy and fortunate adventure, and who implores your aid and protection."

"Prince," she replied, "the kingdom of Bengal, in which you now are, will afford you all the hospitality and assistance you may require. My father, the Rajah, built this palace not far from his capital for the sake of the country air. Of this place I am absolute mistress and I bid you welcome. At the same time, though I much desire to know by what means you have arrived here from such a far country as Persia, and by what magic you have evaded the vigilance of my guards, I am convinced that you must be in need of rest and refreshment. I will, therefore, direct my attendants to show you to an apartment where you may obtain both before answering any of the questions which I am dying to put."

Her attendants, though naturally surprised at the sight of the prince in their midst, at once carried out her commands. He was conducted to a handsome room, where, after he had been given the refreshment of which he was so much in need, he slept soundly until morning.

The princess took great pains with her toilet the next day, and changed her mind so often as to what she would wear, and, generally, gave so much trouble to her attendants that they plainly perceived what a favorable impression the stranger must have produced.

When her mirror assured her that never had she appeared so charming, she sent for the prince and expressed a desire to hear

what strange adventure had caused his sudden appearance of the night before.

The prince was only too pleased to relate the story of the enchanted horse and all that had befallen him since he had mounted it. He concluded by thanking her for the kind and hospitable manner in which she had received him. Then he declared that it would now be his reluctant duty to return without delay, and relieve the anxiety of his father.

The princess urged him to stay a short time longer, as her guest, to see a little of the kingdom of Bengal, where he had so unexpectedly arrived and of which he would then be better able to give an account of his return to Persia.

The prince could hardly refuse such a request from such a charming princess. And so he put off his return from day to day and from week to week, while the princess entertained him with feasts, concerts, hunting parties, and every other form of amusement she could think of. In this way, the time flew so fast that the prince was surprised and ashamed when one day he realized that two months had passed, during which time his father must have either suffered the greatest possible anxiety, or else have concluded that his son was dead. Not another day would he consent to remain at the palace. And yet, he asked, how could he tear himself away from his adorable princess?

The princess made no reply to this, beyond casting down her eyes and blushing. In spite of this, the prince went on to ask whether he might dare to hope that she would return to Persia with him?

Without uttering a word, she gave the prince to understand that she had not the least objection to this arrangement, although she afterward admitted a little nervousness in case the enchanted horse might refuse to carry a double burden. But the prince easily reassured her. He also declared that, with the experience he had gained

on his journey, he was now quite capable of managing and guiding the horse as he desired.

The princess thereupon consented to fly with him. She arranged matters so that no one should have the slightest suspicion of their intentions.

Very early the next day, when all the other inhabitants of the place were still sleeping, she stole from her room to the terrace, where both the horse and the prince awaited her.

The prince turned the horse toward Persia and, having first mounted himself, helped the princess to mount behind him. Then, when she was safely settled, with both her arms around his waist, he turned the peg, and the horse mounted into the air.

It flew as rapidly with two riders as with one. In little more than two hours Prince Feroze-shah could distinguish the domes and minarets of the city of Shiraz, from which he had flown on the first day of the New Year.

He thought it better not to fly directly to the palace, and so they alighted at a summer palace, just outside the walls. Here he left the princess while he went to break the happy news of his return to his father. Leaving the enchanted steed behind, he obtained another horse, on which he rode; and, being recognized as he passed through the streets, was welcomed with shouts of joy by the people.

The news of his return preceded him, and he was received by the king, his father, with tears of joy. In as few words as possible, the prince gave an account of all that had befallen him, including his sensations during the flight, his arrival at the palace of the princess, and all the kindness and hospitality that had been shown to him since.

"If," replied the king, "there were any way by which I could show my gratitude to this lady, I would do it even if it cost me half of my kingdom."

"My father," replied Prince Feroze-shah, "you have only to con-

sent to my marriage to this charming princess to assure the happiness of both of us. Indeed, I felt so sure of your consent that I persuaded her to accompany me on my return flight. She is now waiting for me at the summer palace. Allow me to return and assure her that you will gladly welcome her as a daughter."

"Son," replied the king, "I not only consent most heartily, but will myself accompany you there and escort her with due honor to my palace, where the marriage shall be celebrated this very day."

The king then ordered that the Hindu should be brought from the prison, where he had been confined for the last two months, and set before him.

When this had been done, he said, "I swore that your life should answer that of my son. Thanks be to God, he has now returned in safety. Go, take your enchanted horse, and never let me see your face again."

The Hindu had already learned, from those who had been sent to release him, of the return of the prince from a far country, accompanied by a princess who was reported to be of great beauty. He also knew that she was at the summer palace awaiting the prince. The king had ordered him to take his horse and depart and he now saw a means by which to obey the king and, at the same time, revenge himself upon the monarch as well as upon the prince, to whom he also owed a grudge.

Consequently, while a procession, with musicians to accompany it, was being arranged, and a magnificent litter was prepared for the princess, and while the king was putting on his grandest robes and a feast was being hastily set out, the Hindu, without losing an instant, started off for the summer palace. He reached it before the procession had begun to move on its slow and ceremonious way.

He soon learned the whereabouts of the princess and, appearing before her, announced that he came from the Prince of Persia, to bring her on the enchanted horse into the presence of the king, who with his court and all the inhabitants of the city had assembled in

the great square of the palace to view the marvel of her flight through the air.

The princess did not hesitate for a moment, but mounted at once: The Hindu placed himself before her, with many protestations of respect, turned the peg, and the horse soared upward.

At this moment, the king, the prince, and the entire court were about halfway to the summer palace. Hearing a mocking laugh that seemed to come from overhead, the prince glanced up. To his great surprise and distress he saw the enchanted horse bearing the princess and the Hindu high above the heads of the procession, which, on hearing the prince's cry of anguish, came to a dead stop.

The king also saw and recognized the Hindu, and, furious at this insult to his dignity, hurled curses upon him as horse and riders rapidly dwindled to a speck in the sky.

The courtiers and other members of the procession added their voices and produced such a clamor that it was heard all over the city. But the grief of Prince Feroze-shah was beyond words.

He returned to the palace, where for a time he shut himself up and refused to see anyone or take any food. Then, realizing the uselessness of this behavior, he obtained the habit of a holy man through a trustworthy servant, for he had formed a plan to disguise himself, and set out and search for his beloved princess until he had found her, or had perished in the attempt. He did not know which way to go, but he trusted Providence to direct him. So, furnishing himself with sufficient money and jewels to last a considerable period, he quietly left his father's palace without telling anyone of his purpose.

Meanwhile, the princess, as soon as she found that instead of being taken to her prince, she was being torn from him, had wept and begged her captor to restore her to her dear Feroze-shah. It was impossible to escape except by throwing herself from the horse's back, and this she was afraid to do.

After a flight that lasted through the night, she found herself

early next morning in the kingdom of Cashmere. The Hindu had descended in a wood outside the walls of the capital city and the Princess now had a chance of getting help. In spite of all his efforts to prevent her, she cried as loudly as she could, in the hope that someone would hear her and come to her assistance.

It happened, very fortunately, that the sultan of that country was returning from a hunting expedition; he passed within earshot of her cries, and went to her rescue.

He saw the Hindu struggling with the princess, whom, in trying to stifle her voice, he had half suffocated, and demanded who he was, and why he was ill-treating the lady.

The Hindu, ignorant of the rank of the inquirer, replied insolently, "She is my wife and I shall treat her as I please. It is no one's business to interfere."

But the princess cried, "Do not believe him. I am a Princess of Bengal and was about to be married to the Prince of Persia when this wicked person, whom I believe to be a magician, lied to me and carried me off on the horse you see yonder, which is enchanted. Whoever you are, have compassion on me and save me from this wicked man."

She had no need to urge the sultan further. Her beauty, dignity, and evident distress were all in her favor. Convinced of the truth of her appeal, and enraged by the insolence of the Hindu, the sultan made a sign to his guards, who at once surrounded the now terrified Hindu, and put an end to his prayers for mercy by cutting off his head.

The sultan then conducted the princess to his palace, where she was sumptuously lodged, and received all the respect due to her beauty and high rank.

The princess was overjoyed at her escape and hoped that the sultan would immediately take steps to return her to the Prince of Persia. But she was bitterly disappointed, for the sultan, charmed by her appearance and manner, had resolved to marry her himself.

At the break of day she was awakened by the beating of drums, the blowing of trumpets, and other sounds of general rejoicing that had been commanded in honor of the occasion.

Later, when the sultan came to inquire about the health of the princess, she asked the meaning of all these festive sounds. When she was told that they were part of the festivities in honor of her own marriage, she was struck speechless with dismay. And when the sultan went on to ask her agreement to what had already been arranged, she fainted away—which the Sultan took to be the effect of extreme joy.

When the princess came to herself, to gain time she resolved to feign madness. This she did by tearing her clothes and her hair, biting her cushions, and rolling on the floor. She even pretended to attack the sultan with her fingernails, and alarmed him so much that he left her presence hurriedly, and went to give orders to stop the drums beating and the blowing of the trumpets and to postpone all further preparations for the marriage.

Several times during the day he sent a servant to inquire if the strange and violent attack which had so suddenly seized the princess had passed off or lessened. But each time he was told there was no improvement and whatever change there might be was for the worse.

The next day, since the princess still talked and acted very violently, the sultan sent his own physicians, as well as those most famous in the city, to visit her and report upon the case. But she not only refused to allow them to feel her pulse or examine her tongue, but would not even let them approach her. They came away looking very wise, but shaking their heads and declaring that the case was hopeless and that if they could not cure her nobody could. In spite of this, the sultan sent far and wide for other physicians, who came, looked at the princess (who became more violent at each visit), shook their heads, prescribed medicines for her, and went away looking wiser than ever.

He even sent messengers to other kingdoms, offering generous rewards and great honor to anyone who could cure the princess of her malady. But the result was always the same, and the sultan began to despair, for all this only made him more and more anxious to marry the princess.

Meanwhile, Prince Feroze-shah, disguised as a holy man and plunged in grief, was wandering about the country looking for his lost princess. He traveled from province to province and from town to town, inquiring everywhere if anyone had seen or heard anything of an enchanted horse that could fly through the air, and describing its two riders. The result was that most of those he met and spoke with thought he was out of his mind and, because he was handsome and amiable, pitied him.

At last, as he was making his usual inquiries in a city of Hindustan, he heard the people talking of a certain Princess of Bengal, who was to have been married to the Sultan of Cashmere had she not become violently mad on the marriage day.

At this—for him it seemed that there could be only one Princess of Bengal—the prince at once set out for the kingdom of Cashmere.

Arriving at the capital, after many days, he took a humble lodging at an inn where all the talk was of the mysterious mad princess with whom the sultan was so much in love.

Mention was also made of the Hindu and his well-merited fate. The enchanted horse, it was reported, had been placed among the royal treasures. All these circumstances convinced the Prince of Persia that his lost princess was found at last. The only difficulty was to get to see her. And even this was not a difficulty for long.

The crowd of physicians who had visited and prescribed in vain for their fair patient, great as it had been, was exaggerated by the gossips of the city. It seemed to the prince that it would be the easiest thing in the world to add himself to the number.

His beard had grown to quite a respectable length during his travels and gave him a look of age and wisdom. Thus, he had only

to exchange the clothes of a holy man for those of a physician to be received with civility and respect at the palace of the sultan.

"I have come to cure the princess," he declared. "Many have tried and failed. If I do not succeed you may cut off my head."

Some time had elapsed since any new physician had appeared at the palace and the sultan had begun to give up hope of the princess's recovery. He immediately gave orders that this new physician, who showed so much faith in his healing powers, should be admitted to his presence. He then informed him that, since the Princess of Bengal could not endure the sight of a physician, he would have to be content with a view of his patient through a lattice in an adjoining chamber to that which she occupied.

In this way, Prince Feroze-shah again caught sight of his beloved princess after their long separation. She was sitting in a despondent attitude, and singing, with tears in her eyes, a mournful melody in which she lamented her sad fate in being separated from all she loved. It brought tears to his own eyes and he determined to restore her to health and happiness at any cost.

With this intention, he told the sultan that he now quite understood the nature of the complaint from which the princess was suffering, and that he would undertake to cure her. But, he added, it was absolutely necessary to speak with her in private. If he were allowed to do so, he was convinced that he could overcome the violent dislike that she showed to any physician who approached her.

The sultan was much cheered by this and ordered that the new physician should be ushered into the presence of the princess without delay.

As soon as the princess caught sight of what she took to be yet another tiresome physician come to prescribe for her affected madness, she began to go through her usual performance of threatening to attack with teeth and fingernails anyone who attempted to come near enough to feel her pulse, or examine her eyes and skin.

But the prince, disregarding this, went straight to her, and, bending in salutation, said in a low tone, for fear of listeners, "Oh, my Princess, let your beautiful eyes pierce my disguise and see, in the pretended physician, the Prince of Persia, your faithful Feroze-shah, who has sought you in sorrow which is now turned into joy."

At the sound of the well-known voice, the Princess almost fainted with rapture and relief. But, since the prince warned her that it was possible that they might be under observation, she made an effort to appear calm. At the same time the Prince of Persia, while briefly acquainting her with his own doings and adventures, and listening to the princess's story, took care to feel her pulse and behave in every way like the physician he was impersonating.

He asked her if she knew what had become of the enchanted horse, by which he hoped they might both make their escape. But she could not tell him anything about it. Then, when a plan had been arranged between them, the prince, thinking it unwise to pay too long a visit, left his patient and went to make his report to the sultan.

The sultan was delighted to hear that a change for the better had already take place, and promised the new physician a great reward if he succeeded in entirely restoring the princess to health. The next day the sultan paid the princess a visit. And when the lady, instead of biting the cushions and threatening to tear his beard out by the roots, received him in a most gracious and charming manner, he came away with the conviction that the prince was the greatest physician in the world. He even wished to have the preparations for the marriage resumed where they had broken off. But the prince declared that the princess was not yet so perfectly restored as he would wish. He asked from what country she had come and by what means she had traveled to Cashmere. The sultan at once obliged him with the entire story of the Hindu and the enchanted horse, as far as he knew it.

60

Although the sultan was unacquainted with the use and management of the horse, he had ordered it to be kept in his treasury, as an object of curiosity and value.

Hearing this, the pretend physician stroked his beard and assumed an expression of profound wisdom.

"Sire," he said, "I am inclined to think that the principal cause of the trouble is this very horse itself. The princess, having ridden upon the horse, which, as your Majesty knows, is enchanted, has herself been affected by the enchantment. In order, then, that the improvement which I have been so fortunate as to effect in her condition may continue and be made lasting, it is necessary that I should use a certain incense, the burning of which will disenchant the horse, and so complete the cure of the princess. If Your Majesty wishes to see a wonderful sight, and give a great surprise and marvelous entertainment to the people of the city, you will have the enchanted horse brought tomorrow to the great square before the palace, and leave the rest to me."

The sultan signified his willingness to carry out to the letter the directions of this newest and greatest of physicians, and asked if the princess should be present on the occasion.

"Most certainly," was the reply. "Let the lady be arrayed as a bride and adorned with jewels to set off her beauty to the greatest advantage."

Thus, early the next day, the enchanted horse was, by order of the sultan, brought with great ceremony and beating of drums to the square in front of the palace.

The news had spread through the city that a rare sight was to be provided, and so great a crowd assembled in the square that the sultan's guards had all they could do to keep a space clear around the horse.

A gallery had been erected to accommodate the sultan and his court. At the proper moment, the Princess of Bengal, accompanied

by a band of ladies of high rank who had been chosen for this service, approached the horse, and was assisted to mount. The supposed physician then had a number of braziers of lighted charcoal placed at regular intervals around the horse. Into these braziers he now solemnly cast handfuls of incense. With downcast eyes, hands crossed on his breast, and muttering strange words which much impressed the hearers, he paced three times around the horse, within the circle made by the braziers, which now began to give off thick clouds of perfumed smoke.

In a few seconds these clouds became so thick that neither horse nor rider was visible. At this moment, for which he had been waiting, the prince jumped nimbly up behind the princess and, stretching out his hand, turned the right-hand peg.

Instantly, the horse rose into the air, and, as the spectators gaped after it, the following words floated down and reached the ear of the sultan, who was just beginning to surmise that something was wrong.

"The next time the Sultan of Cashmere thinks of marrying a princess who has come to him for protection, let him make sure that he has the lady's consent."

In this way was the Princess of Bengal rescued from the palace of the Sultan of Cashmere, and brought the same day to Shiraz, the capital of Persia, where the return of the missing prince and the lost princess was greeted with general joy by high and low.

The King of Persia at once sent an ambassador to the father of the princess, who had for months been mourning the mysterious disappearance of his daughter, to request his consent to her marriage with Prince Feroze-shah. When that was given, the marriage was celebrated with much magnificence, and the Prince and Princess of Persia lived in honor and happiness for many years.

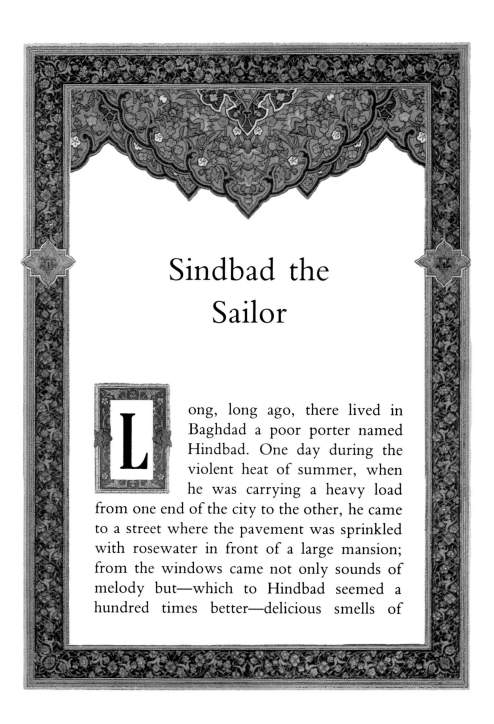

Sindbad the Sailor

Long, long ago, there lived in Baghdad a poor porter named Hindbad. One day during the violent heat of summer, when he was carrying a heavy load from one end of the city to the other, he came to a street where the pavement was sprinkled with rosewater in front of a large mansion; from the windows came not only sounds of melody but—which to Hindbad seemed a hundred times better—delicious smells of cooking. A grand feast was in progress, he concluded, and wondered who was the fortunate person to whom the house belonged. He therefore ventured to put the question to some handsomely dressed servants who were standing at the door.

"Are you an inhabitant of Baghdad and do not know that this is the residence of Sindbad the sailor, that famous voyager who has roamed over all the seas under the sun?"

The porter, who had heard of the immense riches of Sindbad, could not help comparing the situation of this man with his own poverty-stricken condition, and exclaimed in a loud voice, "Almighty Creator of all things, deign to consider the difference there is between Sindbad and myself. I suffer daily a thousand ills, and have the greatest difficulty in supplying my family with bad barley bread, while the fortunate Sindbad enjoys every pleasure. What has he done to obtain so happy a destiny, or what crime has been mine to merit a fate so hard?"

He was still thinking about this when a servant came toward him from the house, and said, "Come, follow me. My master, Sindbad, wishes to speak with you."

Remembering the words he had uttered, Hindbad feared that Sindbad intended to reprimand him and therefore tried to excuse himself by declaring that he could not leave his load in the middle of the street. But the servant assured him that it would be taken care of, and insisted so much that the porter could not very well refuse.

He was led into a spacious room where a number of people were seated around a table covered with all kinds of luxuries. In the principal seat sat a grave and venerable personage, whose long white beard hung down to his breast. This person was Sindbad, to whom the porter made obeisance with fear and trembling. Sindbad desired him to approach, and seating him at his right hand, to his surprise and embarrassment, helped him to the choicest dishes and fine wine.

Toward the end of the repast, Sindbad inquired the name and profession of his guest.

"Sir," replied the porter, "my name is Hindbad."

"I am happy to see you," said Sindbad, "and I should like you to repeat the words I overheard you utter a little while ago in the street."

At this Hindbad hung his head, and replied, "Sir, I must admit that I uttered some indiscreet words, which I beg you to pardon."

"Oh," resumed Sindbad, "do not imagine I am so unjust as to have any resentment on that account. But I must undeceive you on one point. You appear to suppose that the riches and comforts I enjoy have been obtained without labor or trouble. You are mistaken. Before attaining my present position, I have endured the greatest mental and bodily sufferings you can possibly imagine. Perhaps you have heard only a confused account of my adventures in the seven voyages I have made, and as an opportunity now offers, I will relate to you and the rest of this honorable company some dangers I have encountered. Listen then to the history of my first voyage."

THE FIRST VOYAGE

I squandered the greater part of the fortune I inherited from my father in youthful dissipation. But I saw my folly, and resolved to collect the small remains of my inheritance and use it profitably in trade. This I did, and then went to Basra, where I embarked with several merchants in a vessel that had been equipped at our joint expense.

We set sail, and steered toward the Indies, by the Persian Gulf, touching at several islands, where we sold or exchanged our merchandise. One day, we were unexpectedly becalmed before a small green island. The captain gave permission to those passengers who wished to go ashore, and I was one. But while we were enjoying ourselves, the island suddenly trembled, and we felt a severe shock.

Those who had remained in the ship immediately called to us to reembark, or we should perish. What we supposed to be an island was really the back of a great whale. The most active of the party jumped into the boat, while others threw themselves into the water, to swim to the ship. As for me, I was still on the island, or, more properly speaking, on the whale, when it dived below the surface, and I had only time to seize a piece of wood, which had been brought to make a fire with, when the monster disappeared beneath the waves. Meanwhile, the captain, anxious to avail himself of a fair

71

breeze that had sprung up, set sail with those who had reached his vessel and left me to the mercy of the waves. I remained in this deplorable situation the whole of that day and the following night. The next morning I had neither strength nor hope left. But when I was at my last gasp a breaker happily threw me onto an island.

Much weakened by fatigue, I crept about in search of some herb or fruit that might satisfy my hunger. I found some and had also the good luck to discover a stream of excellent water. Feeling much stronger, I began to explore the island and entered a beautiful plain, where I saw some fine horses grazing. While I was admiring them, a man appeared who asked me who I was. I related my adventure to him, whereupon he led me into a cave where I found some other persons, who were no less astonished to see me than I was to meet them.

I ate some food that they offered me and upon my asking them what they did there, they replied that they were grooms to the king of that island, and the horses were brought there once a year for the sake of the excellent pasturage. They told me that the morrow was the day fixed for their departure, and if I had been one day later I must certainly have perished; because they lived so far off that it would have been impossible for me to have found my way without a guide.

The next day they returned, with the horses, to the capital of the island, and I accompanied them. On our arrival the king, to whom I related my story, gave orders that I should be taken care of and supplied with everything I might want.

Since I was a merchant, I associated with persons of my own profession in the hope of meeting someone with whom I could return to Baghdad; for the capital is situated on the seacoast and has a beautiful port, where vessels from all parts of the world daily arrive.

As I was standing one day near the port, I saw a ship come toward the land. When the crew had cast anchor, they began to

unload its goods. Happening to cast my eyes on some of the packages, I saw my name written on them, and recognized them as those which I had put aboard the ship in which I left Basra. I also recognized the captain and asked him to whom those parcels belonged.

"I had on board with me," replied he, "a merchant of Baghdad, named Sindbad. One day, when we were near an island, or at least what appeared to be one, he went ashore with some other passengers. But this supposed island was nothing but an enormous whale that had fallen asleep on the surface of the water. The monster no sooner felt the heat of a fire they lighted on its back to cook their provisions, than it began to move and flounce about in the sea. Most of the persons who were on it were drowned, and the unfortunate Sindbad was one of the number. These parcels belonged to him. I have resolved to sell them so that if I meet with any of his family I may be able to pay to them the profit I shall have made."

"Captain," I then said. "I am the Sindbad you supposed dead, but who is still alive. These parcels are my property."

When the captain heard what I had to say he exclaimed, "That is impossible. With my own eyes I saw Sindbad perish. The passengers I had on board were also witnesses to his death. And now you have the insolence to say that *you* are that same Sindbad? At first sight you appeared a man of probity and honor. Yet you are not a man of probity and honor. You are not above telling an outrageous falsehood to take possession of merchandise that does not belong to you."

"Have patience," I replied, "and listen to what I have to say."

I then related how I had been saved and by what lucky accident I found myself in this part of the country.

The captain was rather surprised at first, but was soon convinced that I was not an imposter. Then, embracing me, he exclaimed, "Heaven be praised that you have escaped. Here are your goods.

Take them, for they are yours." I thanked him, and selected the most precious and valuable things in my bales as presents for the king, to whom I related the manner in which I had recovered my property. The king accepted the presents, and gave me others of far greater value. I then reembarked on the same vessel in which I had first set out, having first exchanged what merchandise remainded for aloes, sandalwood, camphor, nutmeg, cloves, pepper, ginger, and other products of the country.

We touched at several islands and at last landed at Basra, from where I came here. And, as I had realized about a hundred thousand gold pieces as the result of my voyage, I determined to forget the hardships I had endured, and to enjoy the pleasures of life.

Having thus concluded the story of his first voyage, Sindbad ordered a purse containing a hundred gold pieces to be brought him. He gave it to the porter, saying, "Take this, Hindbad. Return to your home and come again tomorrow to hear the continuation of my story."

The porter returned home and the account he gave of his adventure to his wife and family made them call down many blessings on the head of Sindbad.

On the following day, Hindbad dressed himself in his best clothes and went to the house of Sindbad, who received him in a friendly manner. As soon as the guests had all arrived the feast was served. When it was over, Sindbad said, "My friends, I will now give you an account of my second voyage."

THE SECOND VOYAGE

As I told you yesterday, I had decided to pass the rest of my days in peace in Baghdad. But the desire to travel returned, so I brought some goods and set sail with other merchants to seek fortune.

We went from island to island, bartering our goods very profitably. One day, we landed on an island that was covered with a variety of fruit trees, but we could not discover any habitation or the trace of a single human being. While some of my companions were amusing themselves by gathering fruits and flowers, I sat under some trees and fell asleep. I cannot say how long I slept, but when I rose to look for my companions they were all gone. And I could only just make out the shape of the vessel in full sail, at such a distance that I soon lost sight of it.

After some moments of despair, I climbed a high tree to look about me. As I gazed around, my eye was caught by a large white spot in the distance. I climbed down quickly, and, making my way toward the object, found it to be a ball of enormous size. When I got near enough to touch it, I found it was soft and so smooth that any attempt to climb it would have been fruitless.

The sun was then almost setting and suddenly it seemed to be obscured, as by a cloud. I was surprised at this change, but then my amazement increased, when I realized that it had been caused by a

bird of the most extraordinary size, which was flying toward me. I remembered having heard sailors speak of a bird called a roc, and I concluded that the great white ball that had drawn my attention must be the egg of this bird. I was not mistaken. Soon afterward the bird lighted on the white ball and seated itself upon it. When I saw this huge fowl coming, I drew closer to the egg, so that I had one of the bird's claws just before me. This claw was as big as the trunk of a large tree.

I tied myself to the claw with the linen of my turban, hoping that the roc, when it took flight the next morning, would carry me off that desert island. My plan succeeded. At break of day the roc flew away, and bore me to such a height that I could no longer see the earth. Then the bird descended with such rapidity that I almost lost my senses. When the roc alighted, I quickly untied the knot that bound me to its claw. I had scarcely released myself when it darted at a serpent of immeasurable length. Then, seizing the snake in its beak, the bird flew away.

The place in which the roc left me was a deep valley, surrounded on all sides by mountains of such height that their summits were lost in the clouds, and so steep that there was no possibility of climbing them.

As I walked through this valley, I noticed that it was strewn with diamonds, some of which were of astonishing size. I amused myself for some time by examining them, but I soon saw far away some objects that destroyed my pleasure, and caused me great fear. These were a great number of enormous serpents. To escape from them I went into a cave, the entrance of which I closed with a stone. There I ate what remained of the provisions I had brought from the ship. All night I could hear the terrible hissing of the serpents. They went to their lairs at sunrise, and trembling, I left my cave and may truly say that I walked a long time on diamonds without feeling the least desire to possess them. At last, I sat down and fell asleep, for I had not once closed my eyes during the previous night. I had

scarcely begun to doze when the noise of something falling awoke me. It was a large piece of fresh meat. At the same moment I saw a number of other pieces rolling down the rocks from above.

I had always disbelieved the accounts I had heard from seamen and others about the Valley of Diamonds, and of the means by which merchants procured these precious gems. I now knew it to be true. The method is this: the merchants go to the mountains that surround the valley, cut large pieces of meat, and throw them down. The diamonds on which the lumps of meat fall stick to them. The eagles, which are larger and stronger in that country than in any other, seize these pieces of meat and carry them to their young at the top of the rocks. The merchants then run to the eagles' nests, oblige the birds to retreat, and then take the diamonds that have stuck to the pieces of meat.

I had begun to look on this valley as my tomb, but now felt a little hope. I collected the largest diamonds I could find and with these filled the leather bag in which I had carried my provisions. I then took one of the largest pieces of meat, tied it tightly around me with my turban, and laid myself on the ground.

I had not been long in this position before the eagles began to descend. Each seized a piece of meat, with which it flew away. One of the strongest darted on the piece to which I was attached, and carried me up with it to its nest. The merchants then began their cries to frighten away the eagles. When the birds had left, one of the merchants approached, and was surprised and alarmed at seeing me. He soon, however, recovered from his fear, and began to quarrel with me for trespassing on what he called his property.

"You will speak to me with pity instead of anger," I said, "when you learn by what means I reached this place. Console yourself. For I have diamonds for you as well as for myself. And my diamonds are more valuable than those of all the other merchants together."

Saying this, I showed him the stones I had collected. I had scarcely finished speaking when the other merchants, seeing me,

crowded round with great astonishment. Their wonder was even greater when I told my tale and showed my diamonds, which they declared to be unequaled in size and quality.

Everyone was content with his share of the diamonds that I distributed among them. The next day we set out, traveling over high mountains that were infested by large serpents. We had the good fortune to escape them. We reached the nearest port, where I exchanged some of my diamonds for valuable merchandise. And at last, after having touched at several ports, we reached Basra, from where I returned to Baghdad.

When Sindbad finished relating this story of his second voyage, he again ordered a hundred pieces of gold to be given to Hindbad, whom he invited to come on the morrow, when, after the usual feast, he began to tell the story of his third voyage.

THE THIRD VOYAGE

I soon forgot the dangers I had encountered on my two voyages, and, tired of doing nothing, again set sail with merchandise from Basra.

After a long voyage, during which we touched at several ports, we were overtaken by a violent tempest. The storm continued for several days and drove us near an island where we were compelled to cast anchor, although it was inhabited by a savage community of Pigmies. Their number was so great that the captain warned us to make no resistance, or they would swarm upon us like locusts and kill us. This information, which alarmed us very much, proved only too true. Very soon we saw advancing a multitude of hideous savages, entirely covered with red hair and about two feet high. They threw themselves into the sea, swam to the ship, and soon came swarming on the deck.

Unfurling the sails, they cut the cable, and after dragging the ship ashore, obliged us to disembark.

We left the shore and, penetrating into the island, found some fruits and herbs which we ate in fear and trembling. As we walked, we saw in the distance a great building, toward which we walked. It was a large and lofty palace, with folding gates of ebony that we pushed open. We entered the courtyard, and saw, facing us, a vast

apartment with a vestibule, on one side of which was a large heap of human bones, while on the opposite side appeared a number of spits for roasting.

The sun was setting and while we were still paralyzed with horror, the door of the apartment suddenly opened with a loud noise, and there entered a man of frightful aspect, as tall as a large palm tree. In the middle of his forehead gleamed a single eye, red and fiery as a burning coal. His front teeth were long and sharp and projected from his mouth, which was as wide as that of a horse. His ears resembled those of an elephant and covered his shoulders, and his long and curved nails were like the talons of an immense bird. At the sight of him we almost lost our senses. And when, after closely examining us, he seized me and began to pinch me all over, I thought I was as good as dead. Fortunately, he found me too skinny, so, dropping me, he seized the captain, who was the fattest of the party, and spitting him like a sparrow, he roasted and ate him for his supper. He then went to sleep, snoring louder than thunder.

He did not wake until the next morning, but we passed the night in the most agonizing suspense. When daylight returned the giant awoke, and went away, leaving us in the palace.

We tried to escape, but could find no way out. Toward evening the giant returned and supped upon another of my unfortunate companions. He then slept, snored, and departed, as before, at daybreak.

Our situation was so hopeless that some were on the point of throwing themselves into the sea. But I dissuaded them, as I had a plan which I proceeded to describe to them.

"My friends," I said, "you know that there is a great deal of wood on the seashore. Let us build some rafts and then take the first opportunity to execute my plan." My advice was approved by all and we immediately built some rafts, each large enough to carry three people. We carefully hid the rafts.

When the giant returned, another of our party was sacrificed. But

we soon had revenge for his cruelty. As soon as we heard him snore, I and nine of the most courageous among us each took a spit, and, making the points red hot, thrust them into his eye and blinded him.

The pain made the giant groan hideously. He threw his arms about in an attempt to catch us, but we were able to avoid him. At last he found the door and went out, bellowing with pain.

We immediately ran to the shore where our rafts were hidden, but we had to wait until daybreak before embarking.

The sun had scarcely risen, however, when, to our horror, we saw our cruel enemy, led by two giants nearly as huge as himself, and accompanied by several others, coming toward us.

We immediately ran to our rafts and rowed away as fast as possible. The giants, seeing this, picked up some huge stones, and, wading into the sea to their waists, hurled them at the rafts. They sank all but the one I was on. Thus I and two companions were the only men who escaped.

We rowed with all our strength and were soon beyond reach of the stones. We got to the open sea, where we tossed about for a day and a night. We then had the good fortune to be thrown onto an island where we found some excellent fruit, and soon recovered some of our exhausted strength.

When night came, we went to sleep on the seashore, but were soon awakened by the noise made by the hissing of an enormous serpent, which devoured one of my companions before he had time to escape.

My other comrade and I took flight. We saw a very high tree and climbed it, hoping to spend the next night there in safety. The hissing of the serpent again warned us of its approach, and, twining itself round the trunk, it swallowed my unfortunate companion, who was on a lower branch than myself, and then retired.

I remained in the tree until daybreak, when I descended, more dead than alive.

Toward evening, I collected a great quantity of wood and furze, an exceedingly spiny plant. Tying it in bundles, I placed it in a circle around the tree. Then, tying another bundle on my head, I sat down within the circle. The serpent returned with the intention of devouring me but, though he watched and waited the whole night, was prevented from approaching me by the prickly rampart I had created. He left at sunrise. I felt that death would be preferable to

another night of horror and so I ran toward the sea. But just as I was about to dive into the waves, I saw a ship at a distance. I called out with all my strength and unfolded and waved my turban to attract the attention of those on board. It did so and the captain sent a boat to get me.

Everyone on board was amazed at the story of my marvelous escape and treated me with the greatest kindness and generosity.

One day, the captain called me and said, "Brother, I have in my possession some goods that belonged to a merchant who was a passenger on my ship. Since he is dead, I am going to have them valued, that I may give an account of them to the heirs of this man, whose name was Sindbad. In this task I shall be glad of your assistance."

I looked at the captain in amazement and recognized him as the one who on my second voyage had left me asleep on the island.

Both of us were changed in appearance, which accounted for neither at first recognizing the other. But, when I declared myself, he remembered me and begged my forgiveness for the error by which I had been abandoned. "God be praised for your escape," he cried. "Here are your goods, which I have stored with care and now have the greatest pleasure in returning to you."

And so, at last, with all this additional wealth, I landed at Basra and came from there to Baghdad.

Sindbad thus finished the tale of his third voyage. Again he gave Hindbad a hundred gold pieces, inviting him to the usual repast on the morrow, when he continued the story of his adventures.

THE FOURTH VOYAGE

In spite of the terrible dangers I had encountered on my third voyage, it was not long before I tired of the land and again set sail with merchandise, as before.

All went well until one day we met with a sudden squall and were driven onto a sandbank, where the boat went to pieces and a number of the crew perished.

I and some others had the good fortune to get hold of a plank on which we drifted to an island where we found fruit and fresh water. We refreshed ourselves and then lay down to sleep.

The next morning, when the sun had risen, we left the shore and, walking inland, saw some dwellings toward which we made our way.

But the inhabitants took us prisoner and made all but myself eat of a certain herb.

I refused, since I suspected some evil purpose. I was right, for my companions soon became lightheaded, and did not know what they said or did.

Then a meal of rice cooked in coconut oil was offered us. I ate sparingly, but the others devoured it ravenously. This rice was to fatten us, for we had the terrible misfortune to have fallen into the

hands of cannibals, who intended to feast on us when we were in good condition.

And so, one by one, my poor companions, who had lost their senses and could not foresee their fate, were devoured. I, who ate next to nothing, became thinner and less palatable each day.

In the meantime, I was allowed a great deal of liberty. One day I took the opportunity to escape. I walked for seven days, taking care to avoid those places that appeared to be inhabited, and living on coconuts, which gave me both drink and food.

On the eighth day I came to the seashore, where I saw some people gathering pepper, which grew plentifully in that place. As soon as I approached them, they asked me in Arabic where I came from.

Delighted to hear my native language once more, I readily satisfied their curiosity. When they left I went with them to the island from which they had come. I was presented to their king, who was astonished at the story of my adventures and treated me with such kindness that I almost forgot my previous misfortunes.

I noticed one thing that appeared to me very unusual. Everyone, including the king, rode on horseback without saddle, bridle, or stirrups. One day I took the liberty to ask His Majesty why such things were not used in his city. He replied that he had never heard of the articles of which I spoke.

I immediately went to a workman, and gave him a model from which to make the base of a saddle. When he had finished, I myself covered the saddle with leather, richly embroidered in gold, and stuffed it with hair. I then went to a locksmith who made me a bit and some stirrups according to the patterns I gave him.

These things I presented to the king, who was delighted with them. As a sign of his approval, he bestowed upon me, as a wife, a lady, beautiful, rich, and accomplished, with whom I lived happily for some time, although I often thought regretfully of my native city of Baghdad and longed to return there.

One day, the wife of one of my neighbors, with whom I was very friendly, fell sick and died. I·went to console the widower, and, finding him in the deepest grief, said to him, "May God preserve you, and grant you a long life."

"Alas!" he replied, "I have only one hour to live. This very day, according to the custom of the country, I shall be buried with my wife."

While I was still mute with horror at this barbarous custom, his relations and friends came to make arrangements for the funeral. They dressed the corpse of the woman as though for her wedding, and decorated her with jewels. Then they placed her on an open bier and the procession set out. The husband, dressed in mourning, went next, and the relations followed. They climbed a high mountain, on the summit of which was a deep pit covered with a large stone, into which the body was lowered. The husband, to whom was given a jug of water and seven small loaves of bread, then took leave of his friends and allowed himself to be lowered into the pit, and the stone was replaced.

I was very distressed by this and expressed my horror to the king. "What can I do, Sindbad?" he replied. "It is a law common to everyone. Even I must submit to it. I shall be interred alive with the queen, my consort, if she happens to die first."

"And must strangers submit to this cruel custom?" I asked.

"Certainly," said the king. "They are not exempt when they marry on the island."

After this you may imagine my distress when my wife died after a few days' illness. I almost regretted that I had not been eaten by the cannibals. And though the funeral procession was honored by the presence of the king and his whole court, I was not in the least consoled. I followed the body of my wife, deploring my miserable destiny. At the last moment I tried to save my life by pleading my position as a stranger. But in vain. I was lowered into the pit with

my seven loaves of bread and jug of water, and the stone was replaced on the opening.

In spite of the horrors of my situation, I lived for some days on my provisions. But one day, when they were finished, and I was preparing to die of starvation, I heard the sound of loud breathing and footsteps. I felt my way in that direction and saw a shadow which fled before me. I followed it until, at last, I saw a small peck of light resembling a star. I continued toward it until I arrived at an opening in the rock, through which I scrambled and found myself on the seashore. Then I discovered that the object I had followed was a small animal, which lived among the rocks.

I cannot describe my joy at this escape. After a time, I ventured to return to the cave and collect a great quantity of jewels and gold ornaments, which had been buried with the dead. These I tied about me and then returned to the shore just in time to see a large ship approaching.

I managed to attract attention by shouting and waving my turban, was taken on board, and at length arrived safely once more in Baghdad.

Sindbad here concluded the story of his fourth voyage. He repeated his present of a hundred gold coins to Hindbad, whom he requested, with the rest of the company, to return on the following day, when he began the account of his fifth voyage.

THE FIFTH VOYAGE

It was not long before the peaceful and pleasant life I led became dull. This time I built a vessel of my own, on which I took several other merchants as passengers. We set sail with a fair wind and a rich cargo. The first place at which we stopped was a desert island, where we found the egg of a roc, as large as the one I spoke of on a former occasion. It contained a small roc, almost hatched. Its beak had begun to pierce the shell. My companions, in spite of my advice, broke open the egg with hatchets, and roasted the young bird, bit by bit.

They had scarcely finished their meal when two immense clouds appeared in the air at a considerable distance. The captain realized that the parents of the young roc were coming, and warned us to reembark as quickly as possible, to escape the danger that threatened us. We took his advice and set sail immediately.

The two rocs approached, uttering the most terrible screams, which they redoubled on finding their egg broken and their young one destroyed. Then they flew away toward the mountains from where they had come. We hoped we had seen the last of them.

But they soon returned, each with an enormous piece of rock in its claws, which, when they were directly over our ship, they let

91

fall. Our ship was smashed. Everyone on board, with the exception of myself, was either crushed to death or drowned.

I was under water for some time, but, coming to the surface, was able to seize a piece of wreckage with the aid of which I reached an island.

When I had rested awhile, I proceeded farther inland and was charmed by the beauty of all I saw. I ate the ripe fruit which hung from the trees on every side and drank from the crystal streams.

When night came I lay down to rest on a mossy bank. When the sun rose I continued on my way until I came to a little rivulet, beside which I saw an aged man seated.

I saluted him and asked what he was doing there. Instead of answering, he made signs to me to take him on my shoulders and cross the brook, making me understand that he wanted to gather some fruit on the other side.

Accordingly, taking him on my back I waded through the stream. When I had reached the other side, I stooped for him to alight. Instead he clambered onto my shoulders, crossed his legs round my neck, and gripped me so tightly around the throat that I was nearly strangled and fell to the ground.

But he still stayed on my shoulders and kicked me so hard that I was forced to rise. He then made me walk under some trees, the fruit of which he gathered and ate. He didn't release his hold during the day. And at night he laid himself on the ground, still clinging to my neck.

From this time forward I was his beast of burden. All attempts to dislodge him were in vain. Finally, one day, I chanced to find on the ground several dried gourds that had fallen from the tree that bore them. I took a large one, and, after having cleared it out I squeezed into it the juice of several bunches of grapes, which the island produced in great abundance. This I left in a particular spot for some days, when, returning, I found the juice changed into wine.

I drank some of it and it had such an exhilarating effect that, in spite of my burden, I began to dance and sing. Noticing this, the old man indicated that he also wished to taste the liquor. He liked it so well that he emptied the gourd. The wine went almost immediately to his head, and he began to sway to and fro on my shoulders. Before long his grasp relaxed and I was able to throw him to the ground.

I was delighted to have got rid of this old man and I set out toward the seashore, where I met some people who belonged to a

vessel that had anchored there to get fresh water. They were much astonished at seeing me and hearing the account of my adventure.

"You had fallen," they said, "into the hands of the Old Man of the Sea, and you are the first of his captives whom he has not strangled sooner or later. Because of him the sailors and merchants who land here never dare approach except in a strong body."

They then took me to their ship and I sailed with them. In a few days we anchored in the harbor of a large city.

One of the merchants on the ship had become very friendly with me. When we landed he gave me a large sack, and then introduced me to some others who were also furnished with sacks. He said, "Follow these people, and do as they do."

We set off together and arrived at a large forest of coconut trees, the trunks of which were so smooth that it was impossible for any to climb, except the monkeys who lived among the branches.

My companions collected stones which they threw at the monkeys, who retaliated by hurling coconuts at us. In this way, we easily obtained enough to fill our sacks.

By selling these coconuts to merchants in the city, in the course of time I made a considerable sum.

I then obtained a passage in a ship that called for a cargo of coconuts. It was bound for the Island of Kamari, which was celebrated for its pearl fishery.

Here I hired divers and was fortunate to obtain a number of fine pearls, with which I again set sail. I landed in Basra, having still further increased my riches, a tenth part of which I bestowed in charity, as was now my custom on returning from a voyage.

At the end of this narrative Sindbad, as usual, gave a hundred pieces of gold to Hindbad, who left with all the other guests. The same party returned the next day. After their host had fed them in as sumptuous a manner as on the preceding days, he began the account of his sixth voyage.

THE SIXTH VOYAGE

About a year after my return from my fifth voyage, I again embarked on a ship, the captain of which intended to make a long voyage.

Long indeed it proved to be, for the captain and pilot lost their way and did not know how to navigate. When, at last, the captain discovered our whereabouts, he threw his turban on the deck, tore his beard, and beat his head like a man distraught.

On being asked the reason for this behavior, he replied, "We are in the greatest peril. A rapid current is pushing the ship, and we shall all perish in less than a quarter of an hour. Pray Allah to deliver us from this dreadful danger. Nothing can save us unless He takes pity on us."

He then gave orders to hoist more sail, but the ropes broke in the attempt. The ship became quite unmanageable and was dashed by the current against a rock, where it split into pieces. Nevertheless, we had time to remove our provisions, as well as the most valuable part of the cargo.

When we were assembled on the shore the captain said, "Allah's will be done. Here we may dig our graves for we are in a place so desolate that no one else cast on this shore has ever returned to his own home."

We were at the foot of a mountain, which formed part of an island. The coast was covered with wreckage and all kinds of valuable merchandise in bales and chests that had been thrown up by the sea. Indeed, if we could have lived on gold or jewels, all might have been well. As it was, starvation was bound to overcome us before very long.

There was, however, one strange thing about the place: a river of fresh water ran from the sea and disappeared into a cavern in the mountain.

We remained on the shore in a hopeless condition. The mountain was too steep to climb and so we were without any means of escape. The fate we feared gradually overcame us. Those who died first were buried by the others. I had the dismal job of burying my last companion, for I had eaten more sparingly of my share of the stock provisions which had been divided among us and so lived the longest. Nevertheless, when I buried the last of them I had so little food left that I imagined I must soon follow him.

But Allah had pity on me and inspired me with the thought of examining the river that lost itself in the recesses of the cave. Having done so, I decided to make a raft, trust myself to the current, and see where it would take me. If I perished, I would change only the manner of my death.

I set to work at once and made a strong framework of wood bound with rope, of which there was an abundance scattered about the shore. I then selected from among the wreckage the chests containing the most gold and valuable jewels. When I had carefully stowed these to balance the raft, I embarked on my vessel, guiding it with the little oar I had made.

The current carried me under the vault of the cavern and I soon found myself in darkness. I rowed, for what seemed to be days, without seeing a single ray of light.

During this time, I ate the last of my hoarded stock of provisions. I then either fell asleep or became unconscious. When I came to I

 96

was astonished to find myself in open country, near a bank of the river, to which my raft was fastened, and surrounded by a number of black men.

I felt so overcome with joy that I could scarcely believe myself awake. At last, convinced that my deliverance was not a dream, I gave thanks aloud; and one of the men who understood Arabic, advanced and said, "Do not be alarmed at the sight of us. The river that issues from yonder mountain is that from which we get water for our fields. When we saw your raft being borne toward us, we swam to it, and guided it to shore. And now I beg you to tell us from where you came."

I replied, "I will do so, with pleasure, when I have eaten. I am at the point of starvation."

I satisfied my hunger and then proceeded to satisfy their curiosity. They then said they must take me to their king. So, having procured a horse for me, they pulled my raft ashore and followed me with it on their shoulders to the city of Serendib, where their king received me with great kindness.

To him I related all that had befallen me. He was so pleased with the story of my adventures that he ordered it to be written in letters of gold and preserved among the archives of his kingdom. The raft was then produced and, prostrating myself before him, I said: "If Your Majesty will honor me by accepting my cargo, it is all at your disposal."

But, although he smiled and appeared pleased, he refused my offer, and said that when I left his kingdom I should take with me proof of his regard.

After I had spent some days exploring the city and its surroundings, I begged to be allowed to return to my own country. The king not only gave me permission, together with a gift of great value, but also did me the high honor of entrusting me with a letter and gifts for the Caliph Haroun Alraschid. These gifts included a vase made of a single ruby, filled with pearls, and a female slave of marvelous beauty who wore jewels worth a king's ransom.

After a long but pleasant voyage, we landed at Basra, from where I returned to Baghdad. At once I presented the letter and the gifts of the King of Serendib to the caliph, who, after he had asked me a number of questions about the country from which I had returned, dismissed me with a handsome present.

Sindbad here finished his tale, and his visitors left, Hindbad, as usual, receiving his hundred gold pieces. The guests and the porter returned on the following day and Sindbad began to tell of his seventh and last voyage.

THE SEVENTH AND LAST VOYAGE

I now decided, since I was past the prime of life, to go to sea no more, but to enjoy a pleasant and restful existence at home.

But one day the caliph sent for me.

"Sindbad," he said, "I want you to do me a service. You must go once more to the King of Serendib with my answer and presents. It is only right that I should reply properly to him."

"Commander of the Faithful," I replied, "I humbly beg you to consider that I am exhausted by all I have undergone in my six voyages. I have even made a vow never again to leave Baghdad."

I then related the long tale of my adventures. When I had finished, the caliph said, "I confess that these are extraordinary adventures. Nevertheless, they must not prevent you from making the voyage I propose, which is only to the island of Serendib. You must agree that it would be wrong if I remained under obligation to the king of that island."

Since it was clear that the caliph was insisting that I go, I signified that I was ready to obey his commands. He then provided me with a thousand pieces of gold to cover the expenses of the voyage.

In a few days, having received the presents from the caliph, together with a letter written by his own hand, I set off for Basra,

where I embarked and, after a pleasant voyage, arrived at the island of Serendib.

I soon obtained an audience with the king, who showed pleasure at the sight of me. "Welcome, Sindbad," he said. "I assure you I have often thought of you since your departure. Blessed be this day in which I see you again."

After thanking the king for his kindness, I delivered the caliph's letter and presents, which he received with great pleasure.

The caliph had sent the king a complete bolt of gold tissue, fifty robes of a very rare material, a hundred more of the finest white linen, a bolt of crimson velvet, and another of a different pattern and color. In addition, he sent a vase of agate, carved in the most wonderful manner.

Soon after this, I requested leave to depart, which the king granted, at the same time giving me a handsome present. I then reembarked. But three or four days after we set sail we were attacked by pirates, who quickly made themselves masters of our vessel. Those who tried to resist lost their lives. I and all those who had the prudence to submit quietly were made slaves. After they had stripped us and clothed us in rags instead of our own garments, the pirates bent their course toward a distant island, where they sold us.

I was purchased by a rich merchant who took me home with him. Some days later he asked me if I could shoot with a bow and arrow.

I replied that I had practiced that sport in my youth and that I did not think I had entirely lost my skill. He then gave me a bow and some arrows and, making me mount behind him on an elephant, took me to a vast forest some hours' journey from the city. We went a great way into the forest, until the merchant came to a particular spot, where he made me alight. Then he showed me a large tree. "Climb that tree," he said, "and shoot at the elephants

that pass under it. There are many of these animals in this forest. If one should fall, come and let me know."

He then left me some provisions and returned to the city.

During the first night no elephants came. But the next day, as soon as the sun had risen, a great number made their appearance. I shot many arrows at them and at last one fell. The others immediately ran away, and left me at liberty to go and inform my master of my success.

He praised me and, returning with me, we dug a pit and buried the elephant, so that the body might rot and the tusks be more easily secured.

I continued my new occupation for two months. Not a day passed on which I did not kill an elephant. But one day, instead of passing on as usual, the elephants herded together and came toward me, trumpeting loudly, and in such numbers that the ground trembled under their tread. They approached my tree and their eyes all fixed upon me. At this surprising spectacle I was so unnerved that my bow and arrows fell from my hands.

After the elephants had viewed me for some time, one of the largest twisted his trunk around the trunk of the tree, tore it up by the roots, and threw it on the ground. I fell with the tree. The animal lifted me up with his trunk and placed me on his shoulders, where I lay more dead than alive. The huge beast now put himself at the head of his companions and carried me to a little hill, where he set me down, and then went away with the rest.

After I had waited some time, seeing no other elephants, I rose, and saw that the hill was entirely covered with bones and tusks of elephants. Evidently this was their cemetery and they had brought me here to show it to me so that I would stop destroying them merely for the sake of possessing their tusks. I did not stay there long, but turned my steps toward the city. After walking for a day and a night, I arrived at my master's.

As soon as he saw me, he exclaimed, "Ah, my poor Sindbad! I have been wondering what could have become of you. I have been to the forest where I found a tree newly torn up by the roots and your bow and arrows on the ground. And so I despaired of ever seeing you again. Pray tell me by what fortunate chance you are still alive."

I satisfied his curiosity and the following day he accompanied me to the hill and, with great joy, convinced himself of the truth of my story. We loaded the elephant on which we had come with as many tusks as it could carry. When we returned my master said, "Brother, I give you your freedom. Up to now we have not been able to get ivory without risking the lives of our slaves. Now our whole city will be enriched because of you. I shall see that you are rewarded accordingly."

To this I replied, "The only reward I want is permission to return to my own country."

"Well," he replied, "you will have an opportunity shortly, for the monsoon will bring us vessels, which come to be filled with ivory. On one of these you may obtain passage."

The ships finally arrived. My master chose the one in which I was to embark, loaded it with ivory, signing more than half the cargo to me, which I ultimately sold for a large sum.

Arriving in Baghdad without any further adventures, I immediately presented myself to the caliph, who told me that my long absence had caused him some uneasiness, which made him the more delighted to see me return safely.

He bestowed more presents and honors upon me. After this I returned to my own home in this my native city of Baghdad, which I have not since left and where I hope to end my days.

Sindbad thus concluded the recital of his seventh and last voyage. Addressing himself to Hindbad, he added, "Well, my friend, have

you ever heard of anyone who has suffered more than I have, or has been in so many trying situations? Is it not right that after so many troubles I should enjoy an agreeable and quiet life?"

Hindbad kissed his hand and said, "I must confess that you have encountered frightful perils. You not only deserve a quiet life, but are worthy of all the riches you possess, since you make so good a use of them!"

Sindbad gave Hindbad another hundred pieces of gold. In addition he continued to show him so much kindness that Hindbad, who now had no need to continue as porter, for the remainder of his days had every reason to bless the name of Sindbad the Sailor.